SHAWN LOVES SHARKS

CURTIS MANLEY Pictures by TRACY SUBISAK

 Roaring Brook Press • New York

For Becky
—C.M.

To my family
—T.S.

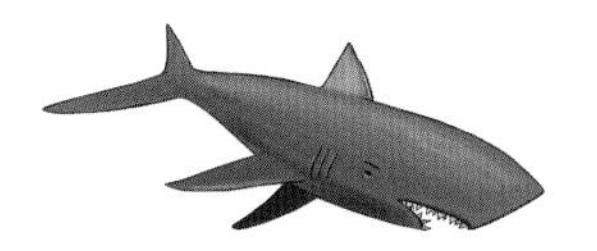

Published by Roaring Brook Press
Roaring Brook Press is a division of Holtzbrinck Publishing Holdings Limited Partnership
175 Fifth Avenue, New York, New York 10010
mackids.com

Library of Congress Cataloging-in-Publication Data

Names: Manley, Curtis. | Subisak, Tracy, illustrator.
Title: Shawn loves sharks / Curtis Manley ; pictures by Tracy Subisak.
Description: New York : Roaring Brook Press, 2017. | Summary: "Shawn loves sharks with all his heart, so when his nemesis, Stacy, is assigned 'sharks' for the big class project, Shawn is not happy"—Provided by publisher.
Identifiers: LCCN 2016025026 | ISBN 9781626721340 (hardback)
Subjects: | CYAC: Schools—Fiction. | Sharks—Fiction. | Friendship—Fiction. | Imagination—Fiction. | BISAC: JUVENILE FICTION / Animals / Marine Life. | JUVENILE FICTION / Social Issues / Friendship. | JUVENILE FICTION / General.
Classification: LCC PZ7.1.M365 Sh 2017 | DDC [E]—dc23
LC record available at https://lccn.loc.gov/2016025026

Our books may be purchased in bulk for promotional, educational, or business use.
Please contact your local bookseller or the Macmillan Corporate and Premium Sales Department at (800) 221-7945 ext. 5442 or by e-mail at MacmillanSpecialMarkets@macmillan.com.

First edition 2017
Book design by Roberta Pressel
Printed in China by Toppan Leefung Printing Ltd.,
Dongguan City, Guangdong Province

1 3 5 7 9 10 8 6 4 2

Shawn loved sharks.

He loved their streamlined shape. He loved their dark, blank eyes. He loved their big mouths full of sharp teeth. He loved how they could sneak up on something tasty and grab it with one big bite.

Shawn thought about sharks all the time.

When Shawn ate, he opened his mouth wide for each bite.

Shawn watched shark videos, knew all the shark movies by heart, and had 127 shark books.

At recess, Shawn opened his mouth very wide and chased the other kids—especially Stacy, who screamed the loudest.

Shawn loved how everything got out of the way of a shark.

On Monday, Ms. Mitchell told the class they would each learn about a different predator. Shawn leaped out of his chair and yelled,

The animal Shawn picked was not Shark. It wasn't even Lion or Tiger or Grizzly Bear or Orca or Tyrannosaurus Rex.

It was Leopard Seal.

"A seal?!" whispered Shawn.

Great White Shark was picked by . . . Stacy.

Shawn said,

He said,

e said,

Stacy shook her head. She smiled. She opened her mouth wide. Very wide.

At home, Shawn looked through his shark books hoping that what he remembered about sharks and seals was wrong.

It wasn't wrong.

He hoped Stacy wouldn't find out.

She found out.

Tuesday on the playground,
Stacy leaned close and said,
Did you know that sharks eat seals?
Shawn nodded.
But not if they can't catch them!

Stacy opened her mouth very wide and ran as fast as she could, but she couldn't catch Shawn.

Shawn loved how a seal could twist itself around in an instant and zip off in a different direction.

The more Shawn read about seals, the more he loved seals.

He loved their streamlined shape and the patterns on their smooth fur. He loved their big brown eyes.

He loved their sharp little teeth. And he loved how they could sneak up on something tasty (like a penguin) and grab it with one bite.

The more Stacy read about sharks, the more she loved sharks—and the more she chased Shawn during recess.

And after school.

Day after day.

chomp!

Until Friday, when Shawn stopped running and faced Stacy.

You're not much of a shark if you can't even catch a seal.

Stacy closed her mouth.
Her dark eyes were not blank.

On Saturday, Shawn
remembered something
about people.

He filled his wagon with 126 shark books and pulled it to Stacy's house.

Shawn loved seals. He also loved sharks.

And he knew that even a fast and clever seal
could never be friends with a shark.

Well, almost never.